a story by **Janet E. Ritchie**

with Illustrations by **Ellen Bater**

Poppy and her Worry Monster
ISBN 978-1-77835-186-0

For All Little Worriers

— *Dedicated to* —
Sascha (Alexander) Christiansen
The Light of My Life

— *Thanks to* —
Dr. Steven C. Hayes   St. Lawrence College
Allan Graphics   Ellen Bater

— *Editors* —
Bentley and Charlie Ubdegrove

— *Thanks also to* —
the Watters, Millen, Steacy and Ubdegrove families
and especially to our original family author
Bud 'Poppy' Watters

Cast of Characters

Starring …
- Poppy
- Rosie
- Cat and Dog

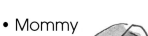

Supporting Cast

- Mommy
- Friends

- Bear
- Elephant
- Giraffe
- Monkey

- Worry Monster
  a.k.a. 'Spiky Blob'

My name is Poppy.
I am 7 years old and I worry a lot.

I worry and feel scared when I hear a loud
BEEP BEEP!!?
behind me.

I worry and feel scared when a
BIG ANGRY dog barks at me.

I tell Mommy that is how I feel a lot of the time. I feel that kind of worry when I'm trying to do school work . . .

OR sitting under my favourite tree…

OR cuddling monkey…

OR when I play with my friends.

My worry makes my tummy sick,
  My heart pound,
  My hands sweaty.
It's hard to breathe.

I want this worry to go away
I try hard not to think about it.

I hide in the corner at school.

I put blankets over my head at night.

I use my hands and I try
  hard to push it away.
  My 'Worry Monster'
  is a 'Spiky Blob'.
  It just stays.

This 'Worry Monster' does not go away no matter how hard I try and I start to feel sad.

I don't want to play . . .

OR read a book.

Worry is all around me.

worry

worry

Worry

Worry

Worry

Mommy says "Poppy we need to find a way to help you feel better and not be so scared and worried."

Mommy thinks maybe I can make my worry be my friend.

"My friend." I tell Mommy, "IMPOSSIBLE."

Mommy suggests I give my worry a name. We sit together and think of a name for my worry.

It could be
Sascha
Susie
Misty…

OR Rosie. I like Rosie.
Rosie can't be **SCARY**!

I try hard to imagine my 'Worry Monster'
as a friend, and you know what?
It starts to work.

My 'Worry Monster' turns into
Rosie, my' Worry Friend'.

She wears a ribbon
in her hair just like
me sometimes.

Once I start to see my worry as a friend, my worry is not as big or scary anymore.

Now, instead of trying to push away or get rid of my worry, I just bring Rosie along with me.

I even bring Rosie to school with me.

I tell Rosie when we get to school, "You need to settle down. I will see you at lunch."

Rosie puts on her headphones and begins to read a book.

When I get invited to a sleepover at my friend Donna's, I begin to feel the 'Worry Monster'. Then I remember that my worry can be a friend.

Rosie can come with me and make me feel better.

Once I am feeling better Mommy and I have another talk. I tell her that now that Rosie is my friend I feel happier.

Do you know what Mommy tells me? She tells me that when she was a little girl she used to worry too, then she made friends with Francis, her 'Worry Friend'. I can't believe she had a 'Worry Friend' too"!

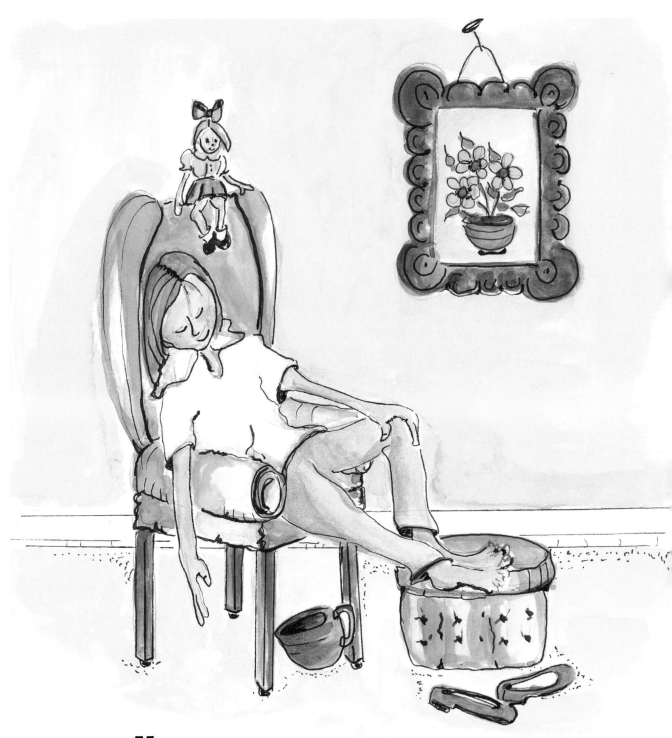

Meet Francis.

It is nice to know that I am not
the only one with a "Rosie".

About the Author...

Janet Ritchie is a professor at St. Lawrence College, Kingston Ontario. It is there that she learned about Acceptance Commitment Therapy.

She has one son, Sascha, who lives in the UK with his partner. Janet has worked in Community Services for the past 20 years. Janet is a worrier.

About the Illustrator...

Ellen Bater is a retired teacher and school Principal. It is her belief that children of all ages experience worry, anxiety and fear. It is her sincere hope that Poppy and Rosie help other children to talk about their worries and feel better.

Sweet Dreams

Manufactured by Amazon.ca
Bolton, ON

34047064R00017